Published by Fitzalan Publishers
Arundel, Great Britain
www.fitzalanpublishers.co.uk

ISBN – 978-0-9576961-1-2
A catalogue record of this book is available from the
British Library

Layout by Debbie Kennedy
www.norobotshere.com

With thanks to Peter Martin

Printed in Great Britain by
Pro-Active Ltd
www.pro-activeuk.com

Phoebe Bee In Ambrosia

By Debbie Burchell

Illustrated by Emma Haines

For Poppy

Contents

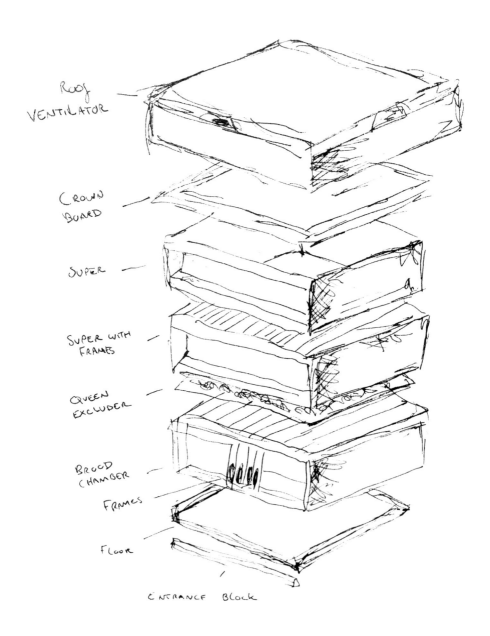

ROOF
VENTILATOR

CROWN
BOARD

SUPER

SUPER WITH
FRAMES

QUEEN
EXCLUDER

BROOD
CHAMBER

FRAMES

FLOOR

ENTRANCE BLOCK

Bee Language

Beebread   Pollen and nectar mix that is fed to the bee larvae. Also known as ambrosia.

Colony   A group of bees living together with up to sixty thousand bees in one hive.

Drone bee   Male bees that fertilise the Queens. They are much bigger than worker bees and have no sting.

Honey   A sweet substance that is made by the bees from nectar.

Honeycomb   Hexagon structure made of wax by the bees. It is where the eggs are laid, the larvae develop and is used to store honey.

Larva   Baby bee grub.

Nectar   A sugary fluid produced by flowers that is collected by bees.

Pheromone   A scent secreted by the Queen bee that influences the behaviour of her colony.

Pollen   Fine grains that are found in the centre of flowers that are carried on the bee's legs to fertilise the orchards and plants.

Pollinate

To transfer pollen from the male part to the female part of a flower, so it can create fruit and reproduce.

Propolis

Bee glue. A sticky resin from buds of trees that is collected by bees to build their hives.

Queen bee

There is only one queen in a hive, she lays hundreds of eggs and gives off pheromones.

Royal Jelly

A substance that is made by the worker bees and fed to all larvae when they are tiny. It is fed to queen larvae all the way through their development.

Waggle dance

A figure of eight dance that bees use to share vital information about finding honey. The waggle of the bee's bottom shows the exact angle from the sun to where the other bees can find the honey. And the length of time they dance for is how far they have to fly in that direction.

Worker bee

Female bees that maintain the hive, gather pollen and nectar, look after the queen and guard the hive.

Ambrosia

Tucked away in the middle of West Sussex, in Ambrosia, a pretty village near a wood, there lived a kindly beekeeper called Will. He looked after lots of colonies of little honey bees. He kept them in beautiful white wooden hives to protect them from draughts and diseases.

Will was a tall, quiet man. He worked hard all week as a rocket scientist, designing guidance systems for spacecraft and researching exploding suns and black holes. But he was at his happiest in his garden with his bees. Will loved to watch how they used the sun as a compass to navigate to and from the hive.

Will talked to the bees every day. They were very good listeners and clustered round him when he told them a good story. He checked the hives regularly to make sure the bees were quite comfortable and that no harm could come to them from woodpeckers, bee mites, wasps and cold. He patched up any holes, treated the hive with anti-mite potion and insulated the hive in winter.

Will understood the importance of bees. He knew that without bees to pollinate the flowers, fruit trees and crops, there would be no seeds, nuts, berries or fruit. There would be no clover or alfalfa for the horses and cattle. The creatures and ecosystems of the tropical forests and savannahs the world over would suffer. The cycle of life would be broken and eventually there would be no food for anyone.

Phoebe Bee

Peeking out from just inside the hive,
Phoebe bee could see the girls
flying back from the poppy
fields. She longed to be down
there, to hear all their news.

But she still had work to do.

She took the steaming loaf out of the
oven. "Next batch ready" she called
quietly, not wanting to wake the little
bees from their afternoon nap.
Phoebe bee pushed her curly mop of
hair out of her eyes and twiddled it
back into neatish ringlets.

She was working in
the nursery making bee-
bread and ambrosia from
pollen and nectar for all the
baby bee grubs and helping
the Matron bee with the
tiny newborn bees.

She spent her day cleaning them up, making sure they
were strong enough to join the rest of the colony. Phoebe
bee looked round to check on the sleeping baby bees
once more, before sneaking out to watch the flying troop
return.

It had been a particularly busy summer. Queen Barbara, the queen of the hive, had been laying hundreds of eggs to keep the colony strong. More bees meant more honey, which was good for everyone.

Phoebe bee was a happy little bee; she never minded working hard looking after all the babies. But she had a secret desire... to be a waggle dancer.

She dreamt of being a part of the synchronised Waggle Dance Fleet.

Sometimes she slipped out of the maternity brood ward to watch the others perform their routines. During the working day, of course, the dance was especially for the purpose of seeking honey. But when the gatherers were all out collecting nectar, the waggle dance team stayed close to home practising their dance moves for the hive convention. They were all too busy to notice Phoebe bee admiring them from the nursery.

"Left, left, shake it. Right, right, shake it." The Dance Instructor bee called out the steps.

"Ok, spin twice. Abi bee, hold your wings out straight. Ready now, on the count of three, the full figure of eight. One, two, three... And again..."

Phoebe bee tried to remember every move.

There wasn't much spare time during the day, as they were all very busy bees. But whenever Phoebe bee got a chance, she would practise her moves, too, learning how to shake her hips to get the right direction in line with the sun.

Phoebe bee had no idea that any bee had noticed her dancing on the quiet, and was very surprised when Lucy bee approached her.

"Phoebe bee, we've been watching you and think you have what it takes to join us as a Bee Search Agent."

"Me? Go out and look for prime honey spots? Are you sure? I mean, yes please! Oh wow, I can't believe it!"

"Could you check in on Monday at 9 o'clock?"

"Yes, of course. I'll be there."

Fancy being head-hunted for promotion like that! Who would say no? For weeks she had been studying the layout of the surrounding countryside and had recently passed her exams. Phoebe bee now had her Bee Knowledge certificates, making her eligible for the next scouting expedition, and the time was now! Phoebe bee laughed to herself. She swanned around with her head in the clouds all weekend!

It was difficult and scary at first, heading off on search flights alone, checking the fields and gardens to find the best spots for flowers and pollen. Her area was up to three miles around the hive. Phoebe bee had flown that far on many occasions, but always as part of the Colony Gathering Troop. This was the first time she had ever been out without a map, with only her internal compass to guide her. Would she ever remember it all?

Phoebe bee was allowed to lead the troop out. This was her first go at being Squadron Leader, and all her friends were egging her on. She fanned her little wings in anticipation, half excited, half nervous. What if she crashed or went off in the wrong direction? She would never live it down.

Finally her big moment came. At a nod from Queen Barbara, Phoebe bee led the girls out with enormous pride. They flew directly towards the sun for two minutes. Left at the second oak tree - or was that right? Phoebe bee hesitated. She bit her little lip. Which way?

Suddenly she spotted the windmill in the distance.

Thank goodness. They were still on the right track.

The Colony Gathering Troop was up to full speed now, zooming over the South Downs. Just past the tree stump where the buzzards nest, and there it was! The bright yellow rapeseed field lay directly ahead.

Phoebe bee was trembling with excitement, but also very relieved. The girls dived into the lush flowers. This was fantastic. They were really enjoying themselves, zipping in and out of the yellow blooms. Phoebe bee emerged from one plant, her curly hair so thick with pollen, she had to shake her head to see where she was going!

On their return, the Guard bees lined everyone up in a queue. Phoebe bee beamed at the others as they waited for their turn to land. At lunchtime, when the sun was at its highest, the Air Traffic Control bees had every little thing in hand. There would be no crashes or pile-ups in this hive!

Phoebe bee had never been so pleased to be home, and she was exhausted. There was a big cheer as she crawled into the entrance chamber. What a triumph!

Smiling, she made her way through the hive, shaking hands and hugging the other bees as she headed to the dining room for a big celebration.

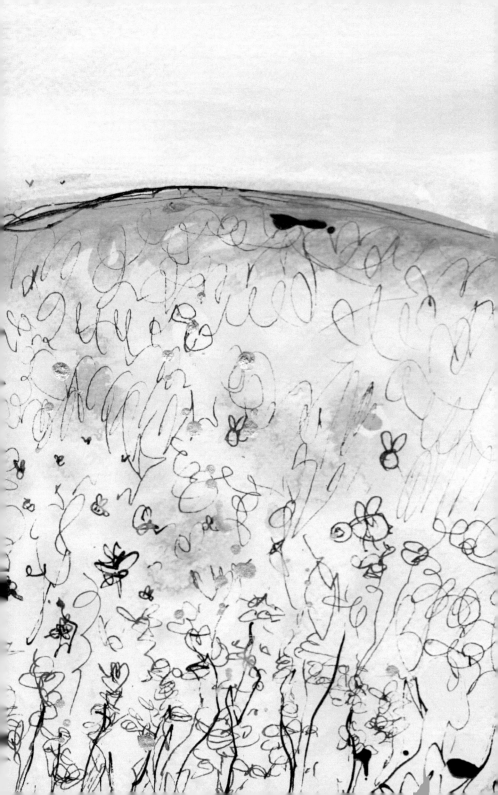

Clover Calamity

Summer had arrived in Ambrosia. All the fields and gardens were alive with wonderful arrays of flowers.

Will was tidying up the bee hives, making sure the little bees had enough room for the Queen to lay her eggs and plenty of storage space for their honey.

Will and the bees lived next door to a cider farm that was owned by Sir Oliver Pippin-Cox. Sir Oliver was delighted to have Will as a neighbour and especially pleased that he was a beekeeper. His bees pollinated the apple and pear orchards making his trees produce lots of fruit.

The bees had also solved another problem. Sir Oliver suffered from terrible hayfever, and local honey is absolutely the best remedy for this.

So these two good neighbours swapped jars of honey for flagons of cider and were very happy men.

All along the banks of the River Arun, there was a sweet smell in the air. Clover! Bees love clover. As soon as Phoebe bee spotted it, she rushed back to the hive to rally the troops!

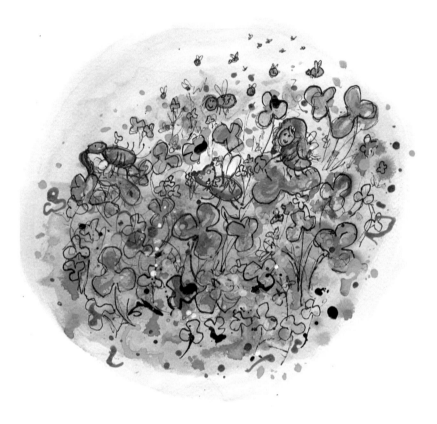

"Come on, girls, you won't believe what I've found!"

Phoebe bee led a big troop towards the river bank. Everyone wanted to tag along. Soon, they were rolling and bowling over and over, playing in the pretty carpet of clover, zizzing and buzzing.

"Yay! What fun!"

Then, a terrifying smell wafted over. Petrol! One of the great fears of bees. The fumes of petrol can damage their tiny lungs and kill them.

With a terrific roar, a huge machine began to trundle towards them. Phoebe bee called out to her troop, "Look out!" But the machine was so deafening, no-one could hear her. It was a big lawnmower chopping down the grass and all flowers. Would the bees realise the danger in time to save themselves? They were having so much fun, Phoebe bee was scared they wouldn't notice. At the very last moment, the vibrations of the mower alerted the bees, and they zoomed out of the way.

"Gather over here, girls."

Phoebe bee did a quick head count.

Oh no, Poppy bee was missing.

The bees were horrified. They began buzzing around the gardener. They didn't want to hurt him, but they absolutely did need him to stop mowing until they had found Poppy bee.

He waved his arms about, flapping like a chicken. The bees flew round and round him until he gave up, switched off the lawnmower and went back indoors.

"Poppy! Poppy!"

The little bees shouted for her as loudly as they could. They searched all over the river bank, in the flowers and the brambles. Oh no, what if she'd been mown down? Poppy was such a happy little soul, flitting from one task to another, never minding what job she was given, and adapting so easily. And now she was missing. The bees all gathered together to discuss what to do next.

"We can't leave her."

"But we ought to be back soon."

"Oh dear. Poor Poppy."

Phoebe bee was about to lead them back to the hive, one bee down, when out of the back of the lawnmower crawled Poppy bee. She was a bit wobbly and wasn't talking much sense as she'd had a nasty bang on the back of the head. So relieved she was alive, the other bees all kissed her, making sure there were no broken bones or wings. She had survived the deathly lawnmower! Phoebe bee told her to hang on round her shoulders, and she gave her a bee piggy-back all the way home.

Luckily, all the honey bees had got away this time, but it had been a very close shave.

When they got back, Queen Barbara awarded Phoebe bee a Bravery Medal for outstanding strength in carrying the dazed and wounded Poppy back to the hive.

Blether in the Heather

One day, Queen Barbara called for a special assembly.

"I have an announcement to make. Next week the whole hive will be going on holiday to the best heather farm in Scotland."

They all cheered loudly!

Queen Barbara smiled at them, "It will be fun, but there will be lots of work to do and I need you to show the Scottish bees just how good we Southerners are."

"Yes, your Majesty, we will."

Queen Barbara didn't want them to let the side down as her cousin McQueen McTavish lived there in a particularly nice new hive. Her colony was magnificent, with about sixty thousand hardy bees in tartan kilts.

She was terribly hive-proud, any scraps of wax were swept up immediately... or else. Her honey was famously good. The posh shops in big cities paid lots of money for jars of her produce.

McQueen McTavish bellowed her daily orders out from her regal throne. Every now and then, when no-one was looking, she wiggled forward on her seat and tucked her hand behind her chair, where she kept a hidden bag of Royal Jellies, which she delicately removed and secretly nibbled on.

Here in Scotland it was Phoebe bee's responsibility to find the best flowers. The hives were lined up all over the heath, to make it easy for the bees to harvest the maximum amount of honey from the heather. The bees were very respectful and would never ever set foot in a neighbour's hive.

Each colony knew its position in the rows of hives because all bees can track down the special scents called pheromones that their own Queen gives off.

Phoebe bee was really nervous when she had to lead the girls out on the first day. She got up very early. Actually, she had hardly slept a wink. But as she took off on her reccie flight, the first thing she heard was a great cry.

"Hurray! Phoebelicious! Over here!"

It was her old friend Rosie bee. They had known each other since nursery, and had spent their carefree childhood days pollen-diving, honey-dunking and waggle dancing.

"Wow, you look gorgeous!" They hugged and danced around a bit.

Phoebe bee confessed, "I am a bit unsure about finding my way around up here."

"Don't worry about a thing! I've already been in Scotland for three days. I know exactly where the best nectar can be found."

Rosie bee quickly showed Phoebe bee the new dance routine, and within ten minutes Phoebe bee had the full waggle dance off to a tee! Phoebe bee flew directly back to her hive, gave an amazing waggle dance display, then led the girls out for a bonanza harvest.

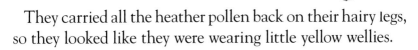

They carried all the heather pollen back on their hairy legs, so they looked like they were wearing little yellow wellies.

The colour of the pollen depended on which flowers they were collecting from. When the poppies were in bloom, the pollen was very black. And when the lime trees were in flower, the pollen was very pale.

But the weather was a bit chilly in Scotland, so the girls generally stayed in bed a bit longer in the mornings and finished their honey milk breakfast before venturing out to gather the day's goodies.

Phoebe bee had been out working hard for seven hours, and it was getting near time to go home when she realised her radar had gone on the blink. She couldn't seem to get on the right wavelength to put her back on a homeward track.

Oh no! Phoebe bee found herself stuck in the farmhouse! She could see the hive through the window, but was trapped inside the glass. She began to panic, and started throwing herself against the pane, buzzing loudly, "Help! Get me out of here! Free me!"

But no-one heard her and all the window banging was giving Phoebe bee a very bad headache. She knew this wasn't the correct procedure in an emergency, but was so flustered, she couldn't think straight. How embarrassing! In front of all the other hives! A big lump came up in her throat.

She began to cry. Would anyone even realise she was missing? She may never be found at all. She remembered Queen Barbara explaining the importance of a positive mental attitude. Phoebe bee began to hum to herself, concentrating hard on communicating with her hive mates by bee telepathy.

Emily bee, one of the older girls, soon picked up the message.

Emily bee was once Head Bee at Beedales Boarding School. She was rather posh, but had a sensible, no-nonsense approach and quickly organised a scouting party. The Search and Rescue Team looked all over the outside of the house for an opening and eventually found a keyhole. Phoebe bee managed to squeeze herself through it, escaping to freedom.

Her heart rejoiced. She thanked all of her rescuers before zooming straight back to the hive.

"Mwah, mwah, so good to have you back sweetie." said Emily bee as she air-kissed Phoebe bee.

Over the next few days, the girls had an amazing time buzzing across the heather fields, although Phoebe bee didn't stray too far from the others. She didn't want to get lost in action again!

Soon, their holiday was over and they were bundled up in the back of Will's truck for the journey back to West Sussex.

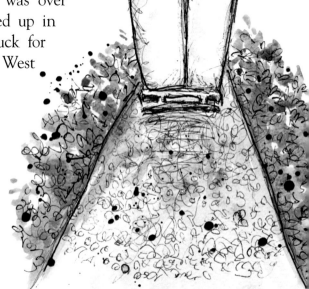

Daylight Robbery

The next few months slipped by very calmly. Phoebe bee was now well established in the synchronised waggle dance team and they had entered the UK display competition. They had passed all of the elimination rounds and were through to the semi-finals. But disaster struck! Queen Barbara was missing. She had been stolen in broad daylight.

The hive had been attacked by a robber beekeeper, which was not only a bad thing but most unusual, as most beekeepers are extremely nice people.

The bees listened to the policeman, P.C. Henry Eagle-Eye, who was talking to Will and taking notes outside their hive. No-one knew what to do, as the Queen always gave them orders for the day. So they all just hovered around the hive, wondering what would happen now.

P.C. Eagle-Eye said they had a good idea who the culprit was, and by lunchtime, Robert Nickalot was apprehended and charged with bee theft.

But poor Queen Barbara 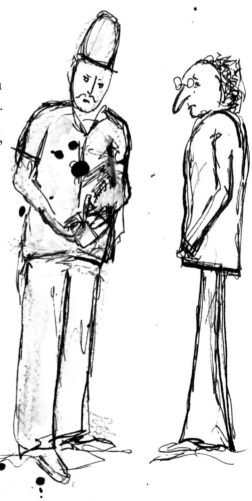 had been wrapped up, posted and sold to a new beekeeper who had no idea he was buying a stolen queen.

It is well known, however, that queens are very clever creatures and wherever they are, will make friends in the new hives, and make lots of honey to keep everyone happy.

So now, Emily bee took control of the queenless hive. She had been a lady-in-waiting to Queen Barbara for a very long time, and had been taught the emergency plan in case of such an event.

First, she scoured around for the freshest eggs that Queen Barbara had laid. Next, from under her arms, she started to produce lots of beeswax with which to build out a honeycomb cell for a new Queen to grow in. Because Queens are so much bigger than worker bees, the cell protruded out like an acorn from the honeycomb. Next, she placed the freshest little egg inside, and asked Phoebe bee to bring lots of royal jelly from the Queen's private larder. For seven days, they fed the little egg royal jelly and watched it develop into a nice fat little C shaped grub. Then, they sealed it over and waited to see if their plan would work.

All the bees anxiously fussed around the hive, twiddling their wings, waiting for the great event. Eventually, after nine days and nights, the wax entrance began to break. The baby princess emerged, stretching herself and adjusting to her new surroundings.

She was long and willowy, with delicate blonde and tan striped markings across her abdomen. Never had the little bees ever seen anyone so beautiful. They all bowed to her and crowned her Princess Beatrice.

About three weeks after the Princess was born, word got back to the hive via b-mail, that Queen Barbara was now living in New Zealand with a very nice colony of bees and was having a marvellous time.

Of course, she missed all the girls back home, and wished them all the best, but explained she probably wouldn't be visiting as it was a bit of a long way to fly.

It was a balmy summer. Each morning, Phoebe bee could see the boy bees checking themselves in the mirror, smoothing down any stray tufts. By lunchtime, they'd be ready to go outside. Many of the drones spent their day either cruising along the hedgerows looking for new Queens or hanging around the door to the hive.

Phoebe bee was friends wth two of them, Charlie bee and Joseph bee. They were always on the lookout for any extra snacks to nibble on. They were so handsome, hunky and strong, Phoebe bee sometimes wished they would talk to her about something other than food. But the boys only had eyes for royalty.

She shrugged her shoulders as she passed them a broken off chunk of laden honeycomb.

Soon, Princess Beatrice started laying eggs, taking control of the management duties, and earning her promotion to Queen Beatrice. There was a great celebration. The new Queen's flags were put up all around the hive and the Bee Fanfares could be heard for miles.

The little bees all showed their respect to their new Queen by working extraordinarily hard, repairing honeycomb, sweeping the floors and polishing up their wings for speedy action.

Queen Beatrice truly appreciated how well the busy bees looked after the hive. She gave off gentle pheromones to keep them all calm, and taught them bee yoga, buzz meditation and the importance of a peaceful spirit.

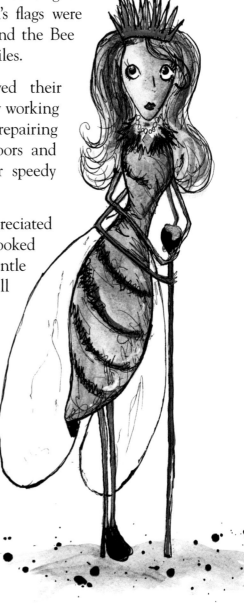

Bee School

Every day, after the Queen's Assembly and the Hive Register had been taken, the youngsters would go off to the classroom. All the young bees had to complete their Basic Bee Education. This covered lots of subjects including geography and geometry. All bees like geometry, especially six-sided hexagons. All bees are mad on hexagons, because its shape fits together so well in honeycomb.

The Headmistress bee was Miss Alsop bee. She made sure that every little bee left her Bee School with their Basic Certificates. She was very proud of the school's academic record, as all her bees left with top honours.

Every surface in her office was covered with sliding piles of paperwork and books.

Miss Alsop bee took all the music lessons and sang along enthusiastically with the students while banging away on the school piano.

Today, at the Bee School, the lesson for Class B was history. Miss Honey bee was explaining the importance of bees in Ancient Upper Egypt. The bee became the symbol of united Egypt when north and south joined together because it flew peacefully over the borders.

This is why there are bees carved on lots of the monuments there. When archaeologists opened the tomb of Tutankhamen, they found he had been buried with jars of honey that was still edible 5,000 years later!

Miss Honey bee handed out a piece of paper to the bees in Class B. It showed a simple Bee Time Line.

Bee Time Line

| 2650BC | Honey bee used on the throne name of all Egyptian Pharaohs |

| 900BC | Honey industry One hundred beehives found in Jerusalem |

| 4th Century | AD Pappus of Alexandria wrote that bees possessed a divine sense of symmetry |

| 19th Century | Charles Darwin the originator of evolutionary theory described the honeycomb as a masterpiece of engineering |

Class B had to create a Bee Time Line Presentation. Some of the bees wore different costumes to illustrate the facts. They dressed as Egyptians, Israelites, Greeks, and as Victorians. This way Miss Honey bee hoped they would remember what a big part bees had played in important affairs throughout history. She explained that even from ancient times, everyone had understood that bees maintain the world's food supply.

Down the corridor, the Junior bees of Class BBB were in their first class of the day. It was maths, and Miss Lee bee was teaching them geometry.

"It is very important that you learn about the 13 degree angle. All the honey cells need to be slightly tilted to stop the honey from dripping out of the honeycomb."

Miss Lee bee held her skinny arms to the exact position. She had been born angular, with pointy elbows and knees. Her limbs made triangles and parallelograms without even trying. She even dreamt about trigonometry, so it was natural for her to share this knowledge, but she could see the young bees were already wriggling in their seats, and it was only 9.30. It was going to be a long day. She pushed her protractor into her back pocket.

Miss Lee bee knew geometry was quite difficult to understand, so she brought out a piece of honeycomb to show the Junior bees just what she meant. She pointed out the hexagon cells on both sides which interlocked like egg cartons at the bottom.

"Would you like to wriggle inside and have a look?" Miss Lee bee asked. They all jumped up, filling the air with a happy hum, and dived straight in. There were rows of little bee bottoms poking out of all the empty cells.

"As you can see, there are no cracks inside, or there would be problems when the baby bees are developing. Also this means our precious honey is safely contained." Miss Lee bee explained that hexagonal cells work so well because they join together perfectly in a grid pattern, which saves not only wax but also space. This makes every beehive very energy efficient.

She wrote their homework for tonight on the blackboard. "Now, Class BBB, please learn this marvellous energy saving rule, as it is very important."

Less wax + Less energy =
More space + More spare time

There was so much to fill the little bees' minds with. Miss Alsop bee watched over them all. They still had so much to learn about the Birds and the Bees, their ABC's and Bee Anatomy. But she never worried. She knew they could do it, as bees are probably the cleverest creatures in the world!

Talent Contest

The summer had been hot and steamy, everyone had been working extremely hard and the hive was jammed full of honey. There was barely any room for all the girls to fit in. It was like a sauna.

Phoebe bee nudged Lucy bee, "Shall we get out of here? I think our work is done."

"Buzzy idea. Let's go."

"Let's play hide and seek. Come on, try and find me." Phoebe bee disappeared straight into a snap-dragon.

"I know where you are, you've bent the plant right over!" Lucy bee laughed. They carried on for a bit, but it was altogether too hot, and they soon had to stop.

Queen Beatrice was thinking it would be sensible if they all took the work in shifts, and rested outside on the side of the hive to cool down.

"Just give me a moment" she beamed a huge smile to her ladies-in-waiting, as she untangled her legs from her yoga position. "Look, I think there might be a thunder storm coming, so tell everyone that they should enjoy the sunshine while it lasts."

Phoebe bee and Lucy bee were right on top of the hive fanning themselves in the sun.

"It's so hot."

"I know, I'm really thirsty."

But even the water that Will had sprayed form his hosepipe onto the flower beds had evaporated.

Suddenly, a big clap of thunder rumbled above their heads,

shaking the sides of the hive. Everyone scrambled to get in the front door. They were all very polite bees, and never pushed, even though big drops of rain were beginning to fall on their heads.

"Lucy, move over here." Phoebe bee and Lucy bee hid under the roof overhang until it was their turn and managed to sip some delicious rainwater before they went back inside. What would be the point of waiting patiently if you don't get a bonus treat..?

It rained and rained for weeks. Once or twice, they tried to go out, but their little wings got soggy, and it's very hard to fly when your wings are water-logged.

The Nurse bees said all the Bee Gathering Troops should stay indoors, as they were bringing too much water into the hive on their wellies. The dampness was starting to make the honey ferment, turning it into mead, which is alcoholic and very bad for bees. The Nurse bees said they had already had six cases of upset tummies in the hospital wing and they didn't want a full-blown outbreak of Bee Collywobbles, thank you very much.

Queen Beatrice was a very good hivekeeper. She made sure the hive was kept neat without being too fussy. She liked a relaxed and happy hive, and kept the front door open to keep the air circulating

But, this year, after all the rain, some of poor Sir Oliver's fruit had fallen prematurely, and was beginning to rot on the ground. This always meant the same thing. Wasps!

The bright yellow and black Jaspar Fleets were soon sniffing around the hive. They were very lazy creatures about gathering stores, and preferred to steal their food from the hard working bees.

Queen Beatrice put everyone on alert. The Guard bees were trying desperately to defend the hive. But as bees die as soon as they have stung once, and wasps can sting numerous times, it was a hard battle.

Will spotted that they were in trouble, and hastily closed down the hive entrance to a very small opening. The bees were very grateful, and the Guard bees soon had everything under control again.

Queen Beatrice suggested they put on a Talent Contest to keep their spirits up. The news soon buzzed round the hive that it was to be held on Sunday. The hive was humming with busy preparation for the big event.

At last it was here. The girls all nudged each other nervously as they took turns to go on stage. Up first, Betsie bee and Katie bee, they did a little cha-cha dance called 'The Bee's Knees' which was brilliant!

Next, some of the girls put on a college production called 'The Importance of Bee-ing.' This was followed by Amelia bee, who gave an excellent rendition of 'Let it bee me.'

By way of the show's finale, Phoebe bee and the Waggle Dance Fleet put on a Waggle Dance Extravaganza that had everyone up on their feet, clapping and cheering. Queen Beatrice said there was no way she could choose a winner, as all acts were unbelievably good. What a party!

Bee Jing

Eddie bee had been studying politics and the environment for many years. He was soon to be the Defence Minister bee for their hive. Queen Beatrice had asked him to represent the hive at the forthcoming conference in Bee Jing. There would be Defence Minister bees there from all around the world discussing global conditions affecting the Bee World.

With his head in his hands, Eddie bee looked despairingly at the list of subjects coming up. Pollution, pesticides, colony collapse, world food supply. A big slogan was written across the top page of the agenda. 'Bees in Danger.'

It was true. Bees were in trouble. There was a strange disease spreading across the world and none of the Scientist bees could work out a cure.

Phoebe bee was helping Eddie bee prepare for his journey. Thermal pants, body warmer, serious socks, she checked he had everything. Most important were his thick gloves.

Phoebe bee stood back to admire him "Here's your briefcase." Hmm, he still looked wrong, a bit undressed.

"Oh my, it's your hat! Don't forget your fur hat, Eddie.

That's it. You do look smart."

They went down together, where the rest of the hive was waiting to see him off.

"Good luck, Eddie bee."

"Sock it to 'em!"

"Safe journey."

The bees cheered him as he left.

It was a very long flight to China. Eddie bee was quite exhausted as he booked into the Bee Comfortable Hotel. There wasn't much time for him to grab a honey snack and get downstairs to join the others for the big discussions.

The male bees were all very good at talking. Only drones were sent to these meetings because, as they have no stings, there couldn't be any dangerous arguments.

Soon, they all started buzzing about. There was a terrific hum in the air. The African bees were a bit scary, and did a lot of dancing around. The Italian and Greek bees were shaking their wings in the air and talking extremely fast.

Whereas the New Zealand bees sat quietly, listening to every one's point of view.

After a few hours, it was the turn of the bees of Britain.

Bracing himself, Eddie bee stood up, remembering that no matter how loud the others were, none of the drones had a sting.

"As I see the situation," Eddie coughed into his hand, then spoke clearly, "All we need to do is apply some common sense. It's time to get back to basics. Wash your hands after you have been out. Don't talk to strangers. Look out for any nasty substances on plants. Report odd smells and strange colours in pond and river water. Be vigilant. Stay organic. And remember, if we bees don't keep ourselves alive and healthy, the whole world will die."

After Eddie bee had finished, there was a complete hush. It seemed to stay quiet for an eternity. Then suddenly, the whole assembly started cheering.

The Defence Minister bees stood up in their seats, banging their desks, clapping and stamping their feet. Eddie bee lifted the roof in Bee Jing. He was a National Hero.

The Defence Minister bees decided to vote there and then. Eddie bee was elected as the President Bee of the World, as he was obviously the most sensible bee to lead them all.

Quite overcome, Eddie bee took a while to consider his new responsibilities and his first presidential decision was to get himself a new fur hat.

Winter Blues

The bees had worked very hard all summer, and their stores were full up with honey. They capped each of the honeycomb cells with a layer of wax to stop it dripping out and to stop predators like mice and woodpeckers getting a whiff of their golden treasure.

They shared one box of honey with Will, for which he was most grateful, and then began to batten down the hatches against the increasingly bad weather.

"More glue over here, please," called Hebe bee. She had been helping the Builder bees block every little crack with bee glue called propolis. Phoebe bee carried a fresh pot of bee glue to her. "That's a fab job you're doing there," she said encouragingly. It was very tough work, this final chore before the hive settled down to face the long winter.

November came and snow fell and fell and kept on falling. Phoebe bee and her comrades took their positions in the hive to keep Queen Beatrice warm.

They formed a nice big rugby ball shape around her to maintain exactly the right temperature. Once in position, they began to vibrate very gently, making themselves into little bee radiators. The girls rotated themselves from the outside to the inside, so every bee had a chance to be next to their lovely Queen, and nobody got too cold.

Also, by huddling tightly together, the bees prevented any casualties throughout the winter. Phoebe was still on

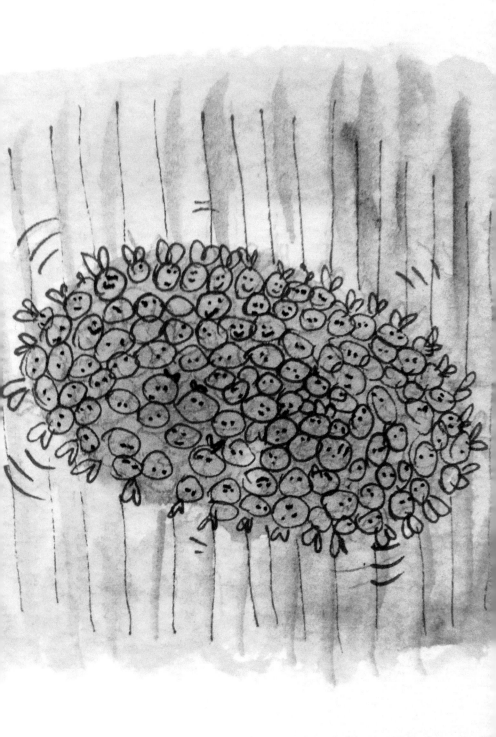

constant alert for any bright sunny days, in case there were any early flowers like pansies nearby, where they could have a taste of fresh nectar.

The winter was long and hard. The snow remained on the north side of the hills for weeks and the ice stayed thick and dangerous on all the trees and ledges. Which didn't stop Phoebe bee and the others going out for the odd snowball fight and a bit of tobogganing.

But one particularly icy day, Lucy bee had landed too fast on the Hive Landing Pad, skidding in on the thick ice.

"Oo, ow!" she cried out from her crumpled position.

"Stay still" the Nurse bees were quickly with her and carried her off on a stretcher.

Poor Lucy bee had broken her leg in two places and fractured her left wing, and was in the Hospital Ward for several weeks, hobbling around on crutches. After her awful accident, the Nurse bees put a stop to any more mucking about in the snow.

This was a hopeless situation for Lucy bee as she had always been a bubbly little bee and very sporty. Even when she was an infant, the Matron bee had trouble keeping her still. Always wriggling off and escaping out of the nursery. And now, with her leg in plaster, Lucy bee was completely frazzled as she found she kept going round and round in circles.

"Patience, patience, sit down and read a book," she was told.

Reluctantly, she went back to the lounge. Lucy bee was desperate for her leg to mend properly, as she was also an excellent sprinter and always won the cross country events. All the bees wanted her on their relay team on Bee Schools Sports Day.

Although considered too flighty to work inside the hive, Lucy bee was a natural for the job of Bee Search Agent and was excellent at it. But now, stuck indoors for so long, Lucy bee found she had a bad case of 'ants in her pants' as well as a bad leg!

One consolation was that it was winter and there wasn't too much flying around to be done. Another was the prospect of the Christmas Pantomime.

The Bee Drama Group put on a tremendous show of 'Beauty and the Bees'. The scenery was wonderful, with feathers and berries draped all around the stage. In her role as Beauty, Kathy bee stole the show.

Everyone joined in shouting "It's bee-hind you!" and "Ooo, do bee-have!"

It really was terrific and had lifted every little bee's spirits for weeks.

Fire in the Stores

Fire! Fire! The alarm rang out loudly. Smoke filled the inside chamber of the hive. It wafted up between every honeycomb frame making it hard to breathe. The little bees knew their Fire Drill off by heart and immediately went down to the store room.

Millie bee, the Warehouse Supervisor bee, directed the bees to get their supplies quickly and calmly, ticking off each name in turn. They gorged themselves on enough honey to keep their tummies full for at least three days. If they were going to lose their home, they needed to have enough food with them.

The Fire Safety Officer bees checked the hive through very thoroughly. Luckily, it was a false alarm. There was no fire. It was just Will puffing smoke round the hive, to have a little look inside. Beekeepers do this to keep the bees occupied while they check everything is all right. No-one minded. It is always better to be safe than sorry.

As soon as they got the all clear, the bees went back about their business. Millie bee was left on her own with the wrecked stores to sort out. What a muddle!

"Do you want some help to tidy?" Phoebe bee could see what a shambles it was. Millie bee shook her head with a shy smile, "It's okay, really. Thanks, Phoebe. It won't take long."

She pushed her glasses straight and set about clearing up the mess.

Millie bee liked to keep the Hive Stores tidy. She had every drop of pollen and honey labelled neatly and entered into her stock-keeping book. She was very quiet and methodical. None of the bees spoke to her very often, which was a shame, because they would have realised what a dear little bee she was. Now and then, Millie bee would watch the others rollicking around - they were all so noisy, boisterous, messy and fun - and she would feel a lump come up in her throat. It was just awful being left out, but she had no idea how to join in. Millie bee couldn't help being shy.

Her proper name was Mildred. She really hated it, and was so relieved when everyone shortened it to Millie. Then there were her glasses, so tiresome, always slipping down her nose. She would love to have contact lens, but apparently her eyes were the wrong shape. Resignedly, she pushed her glasses back and continued with her stock control.

Early one March, before many flowers had opened, the hive was becoming very short of honey. Stocks were extremely low. They were down to the last few honeycomb cells, when a rotten smell filled the hive. A stinky mouse had climbed into the hive and was attempting to gobble everything in the food store.

The Guard bees succeeded in shooing the mouse out but too late - the last few frames of food had already been ruined.

Millie bee had to find rations to make sure no-one got ill. Swiftly, she devised plan. She sent for Phoebe bee, Lucy bee, Poppy bee and Sophie bee to help her move the Special Reserves. Last Christmas, Will had given them some Royal Icing as a treat. They all had a little bit then, and Millie bee had kept the remainder as Special Reserves. But now she gave them out to all the hungry bees as emergency rations. It was an exceptional piece of organisation.

The next day, Queen Beatrice called Millie bee to her chambers. What could she have done wrong? She did as she was told and quietly took herself down the long corridor to the Queen. Betsie bee and Katie bee, the ladies-in-waiting, walked alongside her. They were perfectly relaxed and smiling at Millie bee. This made her feel extremely embarrassed and flustered. She wasn't used to being the centre of attention.

Millie bee curtsied in front of Queen Beatrice, not daring to look up. She could feel her glasses slipping down her nose.

Queen Beatrice spoke gently to her, "Millie bee, you are to be awarded the Best Bee Conduct Award for the excellent way you looked after your fellow bees during the food shortage. The hive would have suffered badly if it hadn't been for your careful management. We are all very grateful to you."

Millie bee could not believe her furry ears. She thought she might faint with happiness. All the bees cheered loudly, as Millie bee passed through. Lots of them shook her hand

and gave her a little hug.

Phoebe bee was thrilled to see Millie bee do so well. She bellowed out "Millie bee, well done!" Tears pricked at her eyes, she was so proud of her friend.

Millie bee floated back to the storeroom, beaming from ear to ear. In fact, smiling helped to keep her glasses in place, even if they had steamed up slightly in the excitement.

She placed her Best Bee Conduct Award right in the centre of her desk. She would never forget this wonderful moment.

Shortly after that, Will brought home a cat called George. He was a big fluffy black cat with a torn ear, a proud uplifted nose and a wonky smile. But George was an excellent mouser, which is a very good thing for the bees and the flowers. Mice raid beehives as they love the taste of beeswax and honey, and if the bees are forever having to repair the hive, they can't get on with the vitally important business of pollinating flowers.

George would sit near to the entrance to the hive like a great lion. The bees respected his presence and, because of his torn ear and noble nose, thought he must be very brave. George never bothered them. Everyone was happy.

Spring a Ding Ding

At last spring came, bringing snowdrops, primroses, and then bluebells.

Phoebe bee stretched her wings. What a relief not to be cooped up anymore. A little drop of nectar and a bit of sunshine, what more could a girl want? She skipped downstairs with the others.

Every day, straight after breakfast, the entire colony gathered for the Queen's Assembly. After Hive Registration, Queen Beatrice gave them a motivational speech to get them all buzzing and finally told them exactly what needed to be done that day.

Now it was spring, sticky buds were just beginning to form on the trees. Queen Beatrice asked the Worker bees if they would seek out supplies of sticky resin to make into propolis glue. After the storms and battering of winter they needed it for repairing the hive.

All the girls looked at each other. Some of them screwed up their noses. Collecting bee glue was one of the muckiest jobs going.

"Come on, girls, let's go straight to it." Phoebe bee needed to get them out there before they thought about it too long.

They'd been collecting the sticky resin for a while, when they heard Phoebe bee and Sophie bee laughing their heads off. They'd got their feet stuck together in a sticky bud.

The more they tried to pull apart, the more they fell over!

"Go on Sophie! If I hang onto this branch, try to fly away."

"Okay, ughhh, it's no good."

"Ha! Another fine mess you've got me stuck in!"

They rolled around until they collapsed with a fit of the giggles. It was hopeless. They were well and truly glued together.

Eventually, the Head Nurse bee came with some special instruments, to pull them apart. Not impressed, she told them to stop mucking around, go to the washroom and clean themselves up. Phoebe bee and Sophie bee did as they were told, but couldn't stop their little shoulders shaking as they tried to hold in their laughter.

Easter! There was a party being held at the vicarage in Ambrosia. People jostled to have their turn on the coconut shy and tombola. Farmer Gus was giving rides on his tractor. The grown ups were supping cream teas and the children were busy on an Easter egg hunt.

A brass band was playing some rousing music. They started to play Phoebe bee's favourite tune, 'Flight of the Bumble Bee'. She knew every note and hummed along.

Phoebe bee had spotted some beautiful flowers. She sniffed around them, nestling down to cover her legs in pollen and to sip at some of the delicious sweet nectar. It was lovely sitting there with the warm sun on her back, watching all the festivities. This, she felt, was Bee Heaven.

At last, it was the Easter Bonnet competition. All the ladies were wearing their best hats, which they had been decorating for weeks. They all stood in a line and the judges walked up and down whispering to each other.

They declared Lady Helen Pippin-Cox to be the winner, as she was the only one with a Bee in her Bonnet! Phoebe bee was spotted sitting in the middle of Lady Helen's Easter bonnet!

There was great laughter and Sir Oliver was so pleased his wife had won, he opened many bottles of his best perry to celebrate.

Phoebe bee flew back to the hive. "You'll never guess what happened to me!"

Poppy bee laughed, "Oh, we already know! Sophie bee saw the whole thing! You're famous now! Been hobnobbing with the gentry, eh? Come on, back down to earth, Phoebe bee! There's honey to be gathered!"

It wasn't long before Queen Beatrice became famous amongst the Bee Royal Families, as being one of the fairest and kindest queens ever to have flown the land. She continues to teach her gentle manners to thousands of her Bee Fans and her wise words are spoken at many Bee Conventions, spreading her love from hive to hive across the country. Oh, life was good! Phoebe bee led the girls forward to pollinate the orchards and crops. She was so proud to belong to this happy colony. There are bees all around the world having adventures like Phoebe bee every day.

So, whenever you walk in a garden or park and the sun is shining, look out for Phoebe bee and her friends around the flowers...and if you listen very carefully, you just might hear one sneeze.

Debbie Burchell lives in Arundel with her family and three cats. She worked as a British Airways stewardess before becoming a chiropodist. When not playing with cats, feet or writing, Debbie likes to spend time with her lovely bees. Debbie has written many children's stories, including 'Oh George, where have you been?'

Emma Haines studied illustration at Plymouth University and won the AOI Images 36 British Illustrators New Talent Gold Award 2012. Emma currently lives in Devon with her family and is available for pet commissions.

We will donate 10p for every book sold to the bee research department in the Laboratory of Apiculture and Social Insects at Sussex University.

If you would like to find out more about waggle-dancing, have a little look at their website:
www.sussex.ac.uk/lasi